THE CHRISTMAS GIFT OF ALOHA

Story by Lisa Matsumoto

Illustrated by Michael Furuya

Published by 'Ōhi'a Productions, Inc.
Kane'ohe, Hawai'i

Printed and bound in Korea

All inquiries should be addressed to:

Ōhiʻa Productions, Inc.

45-934 Kamehameha Highway, Suite C, PMB 343

Kaneʻohe, Hawaiʻi 96744

First Edition

1 3 5 7 9 10 8 6 4 2

ISBN: 0-9760385-0-1

Library of Congress Control Number: 2004112458

Book design: Darryl Furuya

Acknowledgments:

Lee Brightwell
Chromaco, Inc.
Claudia Cannon
Roslyn Catracchia
Raina Matsui Fujitani
Howard Furukawa
Sue Ann Goshima
Steve Holmberg
Sharon James
Michael Kuwahara
Jennifer Matsumoto
Yukimasa Matsumoto
Larry McCarthy
Beverly Motts
Mei Nakano
Stanley Nakano
Michael Paʻekukui
Leigh Sturgeon
Jasmine Tso
Gail Woliver

For *Bryce & Darren*

Love, Aunty Lisa

For *Jenna & Aidan*

Love, Dad

Since the day he was born, Merry the Elf had a special talent for speed. He could run faster than any reindeer, ice skate faster than all the other elves, and when it came to bobsledding, no one was faster than Merry. ❄ Merry's speed was known throughout the land, so it came as no surprise when Santa invited Merry to join his team of Christmas Elves. Santa always needed the help of speedy elves. After all, delivering presents around the world in one night was not an easy task and required great swiftness and speed. Merry was perfect for the job and it was a dream come true!

Upon arriving at Santa's workshop, Merry found it more incredible than he had ever imagined. He delighted in tasting the delicious holiday treats and testing the newly built toys. ❄ While exploring, he came upon a door with a sign that read, "Do Not Enter Unless You Are Santa." Being curious and mischievous as most elves are, Merry tiptoed into the room and was surprised to see Santa's famous reindeer harnessed to a beautiful bright, red, shiny sleigh! ❄ "What fun it'll be to take the sleigh for a ride," he thought. After all, the reindeer could probably use the exercise, so he'd be helping Santa out. Without giving it another thought, Merry quickly climbed into the sleigh, and before he knew it, the reindeer leaped into the air. ❄ Never had Merry felt such excitement and exhilaration! It was a thrilling roller coaster ride in the sky! Merry drove the sleigh *faster* than it had *ever flown before*. Soon the speed was *more* than Merry could handle, and as the sleigh zipped through the clouds, *Merry was tossed from the sleigh* and plummeted toward the earth.

$\mathcal{F}$alling *faster* and *faster*, Merry quickly grabbed hold of his cap, which suddenly caught the air like a parachute. It allowed him to float safely to the ground just as the morning rays lit the horizon. ❄ $\mathcal{M}$erry found himself in a strange and distant land, unlike any place he had ever seen. The trees were a peculiar shape, there were no reindeer in sight and the snow wasn't even cold. ❄ "$\mathcal{W}$here could I be?" he wondered. ❄ $\mathcal{T}$here were no signs of Christmas anywhere. Fighting back the tears, he sat in the strange warm snow, fearful that his foolishness had caused him to miss Christmas.

"*T*his is no time to be sad," a friendly voice said. "It's almost Christmas, the best time of the year!" ❄ *M*erry turned to see Mele, a cheerful menehune who had just put a straw hat on what Merry thought looked like a rather peculiar snowman. ❄ "*T*hat's a funny-looking snowman," Merry said. ❄ "Snow?" Mele chuckled, "There's no snow in Hawai'i. This is a sandman." ❄ "No snow?!" Merry exclaimed. "*How* can there be Christmas *without snow?*" ❄ "Easy," Mele answered. "Things here are a little different from the way they are at the North Pole. Come, I'll show you how we celebrate Christmas in Hawai'i."

Mele took Merry to the Menehune Toyshop, which stood high upon the mountaintop. Merry was amazed by all the sights and sounds. He watched intently as the menehune carefully handcrafted their beautiful Hawaiian toys. He indulged himself in the delicious flavors of the tasty island treats. He admired the hard-working menehune as they cheerfully prepared for Christmas. It reminded him of all the hustle and bustle back at Santa's workshop. ❄ Suddenly it dawned on Merry that things weren't very different here after all. Christmas *was* alive and well. There were *so many* toys and treats, *all* the things that made Christmas special. It shouldn't matter whether they came from Hawai'i or from the North Pole. Merry couldn't wait to celebrate his first Hawaiian Christmas. His only wish was that he could help to make it the best Christmas ever.

Merry's wish was granted when he was assigned the important job of driving the prized Candy Cane Train down the mountain to deliver all the Hawaiian toys and treats to Santa's sleigh stop in the Menehune Village below. *Merry was thrilled* The train was made of the most *delicious* Hawaiian treats, and he was honored to deliver the newly made toys to Santa. Merry couldn't have asked for a better job; this was something he knew he could do. He would make Mele proud, and be the best Candy Cane Train driver there ever was! ❄ Once the toys were loaded, Merry excitedly climbed aboard the Candy Cane Train and started down the track ❄ He couldn't believe the amazing sights he saw along the way, driving through lava caves, past sparkling waterfalls and lush rainforests. He delighted in the unique plants and creatures of this tropical paradise, which was like no other place on earth. ❄ He was the *luckiest elf in the whole world.* He was especially happy to know he was helping to share all these wonderful Hawaiian gifts with children everywhere. This was the best day in his entire elf life! He couldn't be happier!

Merry felt the cool tradewinds rush by as the train picked up speed down the mountainside. His pulse *raced* with excitement as he drove the train faster and faster around every turn. But once again, the speed was more than Merry could handle and before he knew it, the train sped out of control, running off the track, recklessly racing through the village, finally stopping with a...*CRASH!* Toys and treats flew through the air only to shatter and splatter upon hitting the ground. ❅ Mele rushed over, fearing the worst. Miraculously, Merry emerged without a scratch; however, the same could not be said for the *Candy Cane Train* or the *newly made toys*. They were damaged beyond repair. Merry was devastated. He had let everyone down: Santa, Mele, the menehune and all the children who had hoped to receive Hawaiian toys for Christmas. He had single-handedly ruined Christmas. He was a disappointment and a disgrace to elves everywhere.

In the distance, the sound of sleigh bells rang through the air. It was Santa, traveling all the way from the North Pole, excited to pick up all the wonderful Hawaiian toys. When Santa arrived, Merry sadly lowered his head and confessed what he had done. "It's one thing to use your speed to be helpful, but another thing to use it recklessly. A Christmas Elf must know the difference between the two," Santa cautioned. "I've learned my lesson. No more reckless speeding for me," Merry replied. "But what do we do about all the children who were hoping to receive Hawaiian toys?" he asked. "They'll just have to wait until next year," Santa responded, trying to hide his own disappointment.

$\mathcal{S}$anta then felt a tug on his suit. He looked down to see the bright faces of all the menehune children who were offering their own Hawaiian toys. ❄ "$\mathcal{T}$ake our toys, Santa," little Maile said. "Please give them to the boys and girls who will enjoy them the most." ❄ "$\mathcal{B}$ut what about you?" Merry asked. "If you give your toys away, what will you have for Christmas?" ❄ $\mathcal{T}$he littlest menehune replied, "We'll make others happy. That's the best gift of all!" ❄ $\mathcal{S}$anta was speechless. In all his years, he had witnessed many great acts of kindness and generosity, but this outdid them all. This was truly special, a gift of Aloha, one that he would never forget. ❄ $\mathcal{T}$ears welled in Merry's eyes. The children had taught him the true meaning of Christmas. For it was *not* about the toys and treats as he had thought. Instead, it was about *giving* and *sharing* with others. Christmas was not something he could ruin or take away, for it lives deep within each of our hearts. ❄ $\mathcal{T}$he menehune children had given Merry a special gift, reminding him of the magic of Christmas and showing him the spirit of Aloha.

Suddenly, there was a strange sensation in the air, almost a magical kind of feeling. ❄ *One* of the menehune rushed in excitedly, "The train! The toys!" he exclaimed. "They've all been repaired, and they're as good as new!" ❄ "How can that be?" Merry asked. ❄ *Santa* smiled and replied, "The magic of Christmas is very powerful, and when it is combined with Hawai'i's own magical spirit of Aloha, anything is possible!" ❄ *It* was a great Christmas for everyone. The menehune children would get to keep their toys, Santa would deliver all the Hawaiian toys to children around the world, Mele's Candy Cane Train was as good as new and most importantly, Merry had learned the true meaning of Christmas! It was time to celebrate!

Santa and Merry joined in the festivities *"Hawaiian style,"* each wearing a hand-strung flower lei and a brightly colored aloha shirt. Merry had a great time at the Christmas lūʻau feasting on all the delicious food, singing Hawaiian Christmas songs and trying his best at dancing hula. But the highlight of the night was when he was asked to lead Santa's *Spectacular Aloha Christmas Parade!* It was a dream come true for Merry. It would be a Christmas celebration *to remember!*

Finally it was time for Santa and Merry to be on their way. Merry was sad to say goodbye to Mele and all his new friends, but he knew he would see them again someday. He would never forget them and would always cherish the precious gift they had given him. ❄ From that day on, Merry dedicated his life to spreading the magic of Christmas and the spirit of Aloha throughout the world!

❄ The End. ❄

A special mahalo to:

Ruth Bolan
Neil Furukawa
Betty Furuya
Erin Furuya
Stephen Goss
Noah Tom
Laurie Jim

❖

And special thanks to

ALA MOANA
HAWAII'S CENTER®